Our First Caribou Hunt

By Jennifer Noah and Chris Giroux
Illustrated by Hwei Lim

Dedications:

In loving memory of my son, Robert Giroux. — CG

To Chris, I am honoured to have been able to write this book with you. Qujannamiik for sharing your beautiful stories with me. To Shannon, thank you for sharing the creative magic of the writing tree with me. To Ayva-Lin Qiatsuk and Adelle Malaika Nala, nakurmiik for showing me the deepest kind of love and for reminding me to play. — JN

Published by Inhabit Media Inc.
www.inhabitmedia.com

Inhabit Media Inc. (Iqaluit) P.O. Box 11125, Iqaluit, Nunavut, X0A 1H0
(Toronto) 146 A Orchard View Blvd., Toronto, Ontario, M4R 1C3

Design and layout copyright © 2015 by Inhabit Media Inc.
Text copyright © 2015 by Jennifer Noah and Chris Giroux
Illustrations by Hwei Lim copyright © 2015 Inhabit Media Inc.

Edited by Louise Flaherty and Neil Christopher
Art direction by Danny Christopher

We acknowledge the financial support of the Government of Canada through the Department of Canadian Heritage Canada Book Fund.

We acknowledge the support of the Canada Council for the Arts for our publishing program.

Printed in Canada.

Library and Archives Canada Cataloguing in Publication

Noah, Jennifer, 1981-, author
     Our first caribou hunt / by Jennifer Noah and Chris Giroux
; illustrated by Hwei Lim.

ISBN 978-1-77227-022-8 (paperback)

     1. Inuit--Hunting--Juvenile fiction. 2. Caribou--Juvenile fiction.
I. Giroux, Chris, 1972-, author II. Lim, Hwei (Illustrator), illustrator
III. Title.

PS8627.O183O97 2015   jC813'.6   C2015-904620-3

Our First Caribou Hunt

By Jennifer Noah and Chris Giroux
Illustrated by Hwei Lim

"Nutaraq! It's time to go!" Simonie cried to his older sister as he ran through their living room. "*Ataata* is starting to load up for the trip."

Simonie peeked through the window and could see Ataata arranging their supplies next to his snowmobile.

"*Atii*, let's go, we need to help Ataata!" cried Simonie, as he ran toward the front door.

Simonie, Nutaraq, and their father had made a list of everything they would need for a two-day hunting trip, with a little bit extra for good measure. Outside, next to the pile of gear that their father was gathering, Nutaraq read the items on the list, while Simonie looked over the gear.

"Stove, lantern, and skins?" Nutaraq read.

"Check!" replied Simonie.

The two of them had enjoyed preparing for this hunting trip with their father. Simonie and Nutaraq knew that their ataata was a skilled hunter, and they wanted to be just like him. They could hardly wait to bring home a *tuktu*, a caribou—or even *tuktuit*, many caribou—to share with their family and community, the way their ataata always did.

"Do you think I will catch a tuktu like Ataata?" Simonie asked his sister.

"Yes, I think we both will! Ataata has taught us everything we need to know about hunting tuktuit and catching *iqaluit*, Arctic char. I can't wait to make him proud by catching my first tutktu!"

"Me too," Simonie whispered to himself, feeling excited about the trip.

Once all the items on the checklist were accounted for, the kids and Ataata began loading the *qamutiik*, the sled that they would pull behind their snowmobile.

"We put the breakable things at the back of the sled, right Ataata?" asked Simonie.

"Yes. It's less bumpy at the back," replied Ataata.

"It will still be dark for the next few hours, but I know the route to the spring hunting grounds very well. You two can take turns riding with me on the snowmobile and sitting in the qamutiik. Make sure you have all of your layers of warm clothing on."

"Yes, Ataata, we are all ready!" the kids replied.

The trio reached their destination after two hours of travel across the tundra. The sun still hadn't shown any sign of light in the Arctic darkness.

"We will leave the light from the snowmobile on and use the lantern to look for a nice, flat spot to set up our tent. Such a spot is called a *tupiqvik*," said Ataata. "We'll need the tent to give us shelter while we work on setting up our camp and building our *iglu*."

Simonie spotted a large, flat area of tundra not far from the qamutiik.

"Here's a tupiqvik!" Simonie cried, running over to the spot.

"Good job! That's where we will set up camp," Ataata replied.

Ataata lit the stove to provide some heat while they unpacked.

"How did our great-grandparents set up camp, Ataata? Did they have tents, too? Were they made of canvas, like ours?" asked Simonie.

"Life was hard on the land in our ancestors' days, but Inuit were so strong and inventive that they adapted to their environment and survived by using the skins and bones of the animals they hunted to make tents. In the winter they made snow houses, *igluit*, like the one we are going to make today," Ataata explained.

"Ataata, do you think we are going to see lots of tuktu?" asked Simonie, as he helped Nutaraq secure a large rock to one side of the tent.

"Well," replied Ataata, "I often catch tuktuit here, but we will need to be still and quiet once we get the rest of camp set up. It's important for us to have our shelter completely ready before we go looking for game, in case bad weather comes our way."

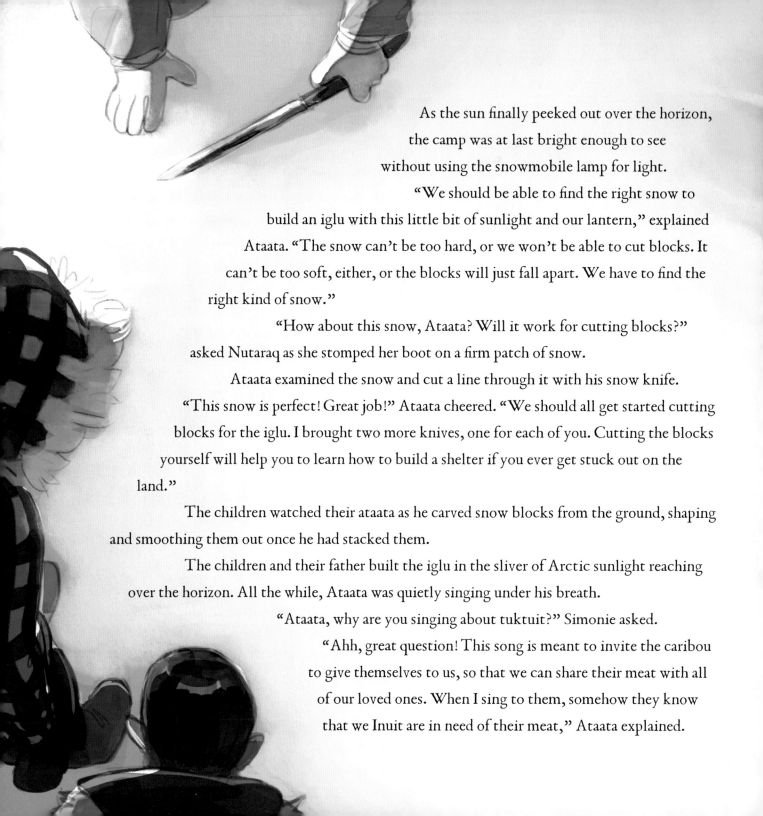

As the sun finally peeked out over the horizon,
the camp was at last bright enough to see
without using the snowmobile lamp for light.

"We should be able to find the right snow to
build an iglu with this little bit of sunlight and our lantern," explained
Ataata. "The snow can't be too hard, or we won't be able to cut blocks. It
can't be too soft, either, or the blocks will just fall apart. We have to find the
right kind of snow."

"How about this snow, Ataata? Will it work for cutting blocks?"
asked Nutaraq as she stomped her boot on a firm patch of snow.

Ataata examined the snow and cut a line through it with his snow knife.

"This snow is perfect! Great job!" Ataata cheered. "We should all get started cutting
blocks for the iglu. I brought two more knives, one for each of you. Cutting the blocks
yourself will help you to learn how to build a shelter if you ever get stuck out on the
land."

The children watched their ataata as he carved snow blocks from the ground, shaping
and smoothing them out once he had stacked them.

The children and their father built the iglu in the sliver of Arctic sunlight reaching
over the horizon. All the while, Ataata was quietly singing under his breath.

"Ataata, why are you singing about tuktuit?" Simonie asked.

"Ahh, great question! This song is meant to invite the caribou
to give themselves to us, so that we can share their meat with all
of our loved ones. When I sing to them, somehow they know
that we Inuit are in need of their meat," Ataata explained.

As Nutaraq stood inside the iglu, cutting the vent at the top through which the smoke from their stove would escape, Ataata spotted a small herd of caribou from outside the iglu.

Silently, he signalled to Simonie to grab their rifles. Simonie followed his ataata and copied every move he made.

Crawling on his hands and knees, holding his rifle in one hand, while making sure not to let it touch the ground, which might get snow or dirt in the barrel, Ataata showed Simonie how to approach the caribou without being noticed.

Ataata glanced over to Simonie and gave him a nod. It was time to shoot at the caribou. A loud shot rang out, and the kickback from the rifle startled Simonie. Ataata's rifle rang out twice following Simonie's shots. Within moments, three caribou fell to the ground as the rest of the herd scurried away. Simonie beamed a wide smile. He had just caught his first caribou!

From inside the iglu, Nutaraq heard gunshots. She dropped her snow knife and scurried outside. Her heart sank as she saw that her ataata and her brother had just caught three caribou without her.

Nutaraq's face revealed her mixed feelings. She was excited about the catch, but disappointed that she hadn't been a part of it.

"It's alright, Nutaraq," Ataata soothed. "We need your help to harvest the tuktuit. It's only the beginning of our trip. You will catch your tuktu."

As the hunters approached the three caribou, Ataata explained, "It is very important for Inuit hunters to give thanks to the animals they have caught. We must show our gratitude and joy to the animal that gave its life so that we could have food. It is bad luck not to give thanks, and Inuit can have a hard time finding game if we don't pay our catch the proper respect."

After the children and their father had harvested the three caribou and delighted in a yummy meal of fresh meat, they settled in for a restful night's sleep.

The next morning, the sun shone enough to reveal clear blue skies.

"Ataata, what are we doing today?" Nutaraq asked eagerly. "Are we going tuktu hunting?" Nutaraq wanted to catch her own caribou very badly.

"If we come across more tuktuit, you can catch one, but today we are jigging for iqaluit."

"Oh," Nutaraq whispered, disappointed.

"Your tuktu will come to you, my daughter. Be patient. An impatient hunter never catches anything, and everyone depending on him or her goes hungry. Let's catch some fish, and perhaps we will spot some caribou, too."

"*Iqaluk, Iqaluk, qaigit!* Char, char, come here!" Simonie sang as the family walked toward their fishing spot.

"I know how to jig for fish, Ataata. We've done this a million times!" Simonie said excitedly as he stuck his fishing line in the ice hole.

"The person who catches the first fish today gets to drive the snowmobile home!" Ataata exclaimed. "On your mark, get set, go!"

Within minutes, Simonie had caught the first fish. It was a big, healthy Arctic char.

"Yes! I get to drive home!" Simonie cheered. Nutaraq couldn't help but feel a twinge of disappointment, but she continued to jig with her brother and father and caught many fish to bring back home.

"Tonight we will feast on char steaks, head and all," Ataata announced.

This brightened Nutaraq's mood, and the three of them enjoyed another delicious meal from their day's catch.

After supper, Nutaraq sat thinking about what her father had told her, that her caribou would come to her. She thought about her ataata's songs, and how he had told her to always give thanks to the animals they caught.

"What if my tuktu never comes to me, Ataata? Am I following the ways a good hunter should hunt? How do I know what to do?" Nutaraq asked, finally letting her frustrations show.

"Well, different communities have different hunting taboos, but giving thanks to the animal and feeling joy is very important to all Inuit, in order to avoid bad luck while hunting. Once you have caught your tuktu, sharing

your catch with loved ones is also very important to all Inuit hunters. The best parts of each catch should go to your mother, grandmother, best friends, and to families who aren't able to hunt," Ataata explained.

"What's very important to remember, Nutaraq, is that Inuit always show respect to the animals and to the land they hunt from. You do this by making sure you don't let an animal suffer or linger in pain. As well, Inuit use all of the parts of the animals we catch, except for some small parts, which we leave for scavengers, like foxes. Inuit would never think of taking an animal's life and leaving it for waste. It is very disrespectful to the entire circle of life and brings bad luck to many."

"Is showing respect the most important thing a good hunter can do?" Simonie asked.

"And being thankful for the animals that have given their lives to us so that we can eat, like the delicious igaluk we just enjoyed," Nutaraq said.

"Yes, you two are learning quickly!" Ataata beamed.

As Nutaraq nestled down in her sleeping bag that night, she decided that she would be thankful and joyful for all the animals that they had caught on their trip, even if she did not catch a caribou of her own this time.

The next morning, the three of hunters began taking down their camp and packing the qamutiik.

It had been a fun camping trip filled with delicious country food, lots of laughs, and beautiful weather.

"Don't forget, Ataata, I get to drive home!" Simonie reminded his father.

"I know, son, you won fair and square."

As Nutaraq rode on the qamutiik, and watched the tupiqvik fade into the distance, she couldn't help but feel a little bit sad.

On the way home, Nutaraq quietly sang about caribou as she watched the horizon, still hoping she would be able to catch her first one to share with her loved ones.

About halfway home, Ataata and the children spotted two caribou in the distance. Ataata stopped the snowmobile and winked at Nutaraq.

"There's your tuktu," he said.

Nutaraq drew her rifle, just as her father had shown her many times before, and pointed it in the direction of the two caribou.

One shot rang out, then two.

Both caribou fell to the ground. Nutaraq had caught two caribou!

"Amazing! You caught them both, and from such a distance, too," beamed Ataata. "Wait until your grandmother and grandfather hear about this!"

Nutaraq's heart burst with joy at knowing she had made her father proud.

Simonie smiled widely at his sister. "Nutaraq, you're as good a hunter as Ataata!" he cheered.

As they got closer to the two caribou, they realized that they were the fattest, healthiest caribou they had ever seen. "Nutaraq, you should drive the rest of the way home. These tuktuit sure beat my first iqaluk," Simonie said.

"No, Simonie," Nutaraq replied. "We all contribute in different ways. Your catch is just as important as mine. I am happy to sit on the qamutiik. When we get home, let's both tell Grandmother and Grandfather about the animals we caught so that we could feed them good, nourishing country food."

As the children and their father rode back into town—full of joy and thankfulness for a successful hunting trip—the Arctic sun set behind the mountains. And in the distance, a herd of caribou travelled silently on across the horizon.

Contributors:

Jennifer Noah grew up in the South, but always had a fondness for the North. She moved to Iqaluit in her mid-twenties. Jennifer has a professional background providing counselling services and developing evidence-based youth programs grounded in Inuit knowledge, voice, and ways of knowing. Through her work in the North, she was privileged to hear stories rich with knowledge and wisdom from many Nunavummiut and wanted to share them with her own children. Jennifer and her family have since moved to Ontario, but remain strongly connected to Nunavut and Inuit heritage. Jennifer currently works with First Nations, Métis, and Inuit students providing cultural programming, support, and connecting them with community resources.

Chris Giroux came into the world during a raging blizzard that grounded all the planes, so his mother gave birth to him in Pangnirtung, Nunavut, rather than Iqaluit. Spending most of his childhood living with his Inuit grandparents, Chris learned about the land, animals, survival, and how to live in balance with nature. He learned from an early age to love and respect the land and his elders and made sure to pass this gratitude for the land's gifts to his own children. *Our First Caribou Hunt* is Chris's first children's book. It captures treasured memories of taking his own children hunting on the land.

Hwei Lim studied engineering, worked in IT and business consulting, and now draws comics and other stories. She has illustrated *The Spirit of the Sea, Spera: Volume 1*, and the Boris & Lalage short story series. Hwei lives in Malaysia.